ORLA'S UPSIDE-DOWN DAY

Mary M. Smith

Illustrated by Jan Lewis

WISHING WELL BOOKS

"Orla," called Mom from downstairs,
"Are you dressed yet?"
"It's my upside-down day," said Orla.
"It takes a long time to
dress upside-down."

"Orla," called Mom from downstairs,
"Have you brushed your hair?"
"It's my upside-down day," said Orla.
"It takes a long time to brush
my hair upside-down."

"Orla," called Mom again from downstairs,
"Have you brushed your teeth yet?"
"It takes a long time to brush
my teeth upside-down," said Orla.

Orla's friend Evette came to play.
"It's Orla's upside-down day today,"
said Mom.
"You'll find her upside-down
in the backyard."

"I'll have an upside-down day too,"
said Evette.
"Let's build an upside-down town."
"It's not easy being upside-down,"
said Orla.

Then Mom took the two girls
to the park.
"It's our upside-down day,"
said Evette, on the swing.
"It's our upside-down day,"
said Orla, on the slide.

Very soon everyone in the park
was having an upside-down day.

When they got home they watched
television.
Dad came home.
He brought some flowers.
"It's our upside-down day,"
said Orla and Evette together.
"Oh," said Dad.

"Have you got time to put
the flowers in water?" asked Dad.
"Time when you're not upside-down?"
So Orla and Evette put the flowers
in some water.
They laughed a lot.

Orla and Evette were upside-down
reading together.
"Come and have some dinner,"
called Mom.
"How can we eat dinner upside-down?"
said Evette.
"Come and see!" said Mom.

They looked at the table.
They saw four plates.
They could not see any food.
The plates were upside-down!

"It's an upside-down dinner,"
said Mom.
Orla lifted her plate.
She began to laugh.
Evette lifted her plate.
She laughed too.
Mom laughed as much as both of them.

So they all had an upside-down dinner.
It wasn't too messy.

Soon it was time for Evette to go home.
"Good-bye Orla," she said.
"I really liked that upside-down day.
What shall we do tomorrow?"
"We'll see," said Orla.

Orla found a big piece of paper
and a thick crayon.
"Please write 'good-bye' on this," she said to Mom.
Mom wrote on the paper.

Orla ran upstairs.
"Evette," she called from the window.
"Look!"

This edition published in the United States by Joshua Morris Publishing, Inc., 221 Danbury Road, Wilton, CT 06897 U.S.A. Produced by Joshua Morris Publishing, Inc. in association with William Collins Sons and Co. Ltd. Text copyright © 1989 Mary M. Smith. Illustrations copyright © 1989 Jan Lewis. Quality Time is a trademark of Joshua Morris Publishing, Inc. All rights reserved. Printed in Hong Kong.